THIS WALKER BOOK BELONGS TO:

_____

_____

_____

_____

To Ninna and Oliver

First published 2000 by Walker Books Ltd
87 Vauxhall Walk, London SE11 5HJ

2 4 6 8 10 9 7 5 3 1

© 2000 Martin Baynton

This book has been typeset in Optima.

Printed in Hong Kong

British Library Cataloguing in Publication Data
A catalogue record for this book is
available from the British Library.

ISBN 0-7445-7811-6

JANE
AND THE
MAGICIAN

Martin Baynton

WALKER BOOKS
AND SUBSIDIARIES
LONDON • BOSTON • SYDNEY

Jane was a knight. Not a pretend knight, but a fully qualified, highly trained Knight of the King's Guard.

One morning, Jane was polishing her armour when the dragon and the jester came by with royal news.

"We have been called to a meeting," said the jester.

"The Prince has got a royal cold," said the dragon, "and the King wants to cheer him up with a party."

"Where is my magician?" boomed the King.
"We can't have a party without magic tricks."

"He's gone," said Jane. "He couldn't make a rain
spell to water your flowers, so you sent him away."

"And now I want him back!" roared the King.

"We'll find him," cried the Captain of the Guard.

"We'll scour the land!" cheered the knights bravely.

"No," said the King, "you will stay and practise a
song for the party. Jane and her dragon will find our
missing magician."

Jane and the dragon searched all morning,
but they could find no sign of the missing
magician. Instead they found a problem –
a wet and watery problem.

They found farmers floating in fields and cows climbing on cottages. They found babies in buckets and piglets in pots. They found turkeys in treetops and kittens in cups.

Jane and the dragon plucked them all from the flood and set them down on top of a hill.

"What's going on?" yelled Jane.

The crowd pointed to a distant figure floating on a cloud at the very centre of the storm. It was the missing magician.

Jane and the dragon flew up to meet him.
"Look," laughed the magician, his eyes as
dark as thunder, "my rain spell does work
after all. I found the missing ingredient."
"What was it?" asked Jane.
The magician clapped his hands together.
"Anger!" he roared, and the thunder
roared with him.

"Well done," shouted Jane. "But now you must stop."

"WHY?" roared the magician. "I've only just begun!"
Again he clapped his hands and blue lightning sprang
from his fingertips. It crackled across the sky and
smacked into the dragon.

"No, no!" cried Jane, but it was too late. The dragon's
wings folded like tissue-paper and he tumbled from
the sky.

"Wake up!" cried Jane. But the dragon didn't
wake up. The thunderclap had closed his eyes
and closed his ears, and he hit the flood with a
terrible splash. Jane tried to keep his head above
the water, but it was impossible. She was sinking
herself, pulled down by the weight of her armour.

Down went Jane through the churning water.
Down and round, deeper and deeper.
She struggled to pull her armour off, but there
were too many buckles. So she drew her
sword and sliced through the leather straps.
Piece by piece her beautiful armour fell away
and she swam back to the surface.

Jane found her shield floating beside the dragon. She pushed it under his giant green head where it stayed afloat, bobbing on the water like a small raft.

When the magician saw what he had done,
his anger vanished and the storm-clouds
melted away. He went in search of Jane and
the dragon and finally found them tangled in
the branches of a tall tree.

"I'm sorry, Jane," he said quietly.

"Sorry is just a word," said Jane.

"A very short word," growled the dragon.

"You made this mess," said Jane. "If you're
truly sorry, then you'll help to clean it up."

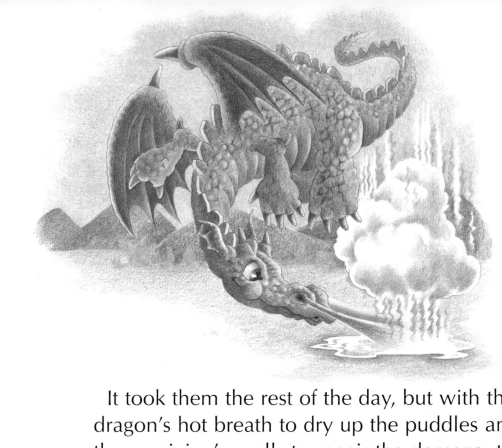

It took them the rest of the day, but with the dragon's hot breath to dry up the puddles and the magician's spells to repair the damage, the work was finally done.

When it was over, Jane pointed to one small rain-cloud which still hung above the magician.

"Can't you get rid of that one?" she asked.

"No," said the magician. "I'm still a little bit angry: I'm angry with myself."

Back at the palace, the party was not going well. The knights were singing their song and the Prince looked more miserable than ever. Then the Prince caught sight of the magician standing beneath his rain-cloud with the rain trickling down into his collar. And the Prince began to laugh. Then the King began to laugh, and so did the jester and the dragon and everyone else in the palace.

Finally even the magician began to laugh, and with a soft splutter his rain-cloud disappeared. In its place hung a bright and cheerful rainbow.

"Magic!" said Jane. And it was.

Jane and the Magician

MARTIN BAYNTON wanted to reverse the traditional treatment of fairy tale heroines with this story. He says, "Fairy tales are tough on girls. Within their cruel pages girls scrub floors, eat poisoned apples, sleep for centuries and are only saved when a handsome prince arrives to sweep them off their blistered knees into a world of Happily Ever After. Not so Jane. Jane saves *herself* and she most definitely does not want to live happily ever after. She wants adventure, danger, challenge – and 'happy' just isn't enough."

Martin Baynton has been a writer and illustrator since 1980 and has an international reputation for his books for children. He is a popular speaker on the creative process of making books and a regular visitor to schools, where he holds workshops in creative writing for both students and teachers. As well as writing and illustrating numerous picture books for children, he also writes for the stage, television, film and radio.
Born in the UK, he now lives in New Zealand.

ISBN 0-7445-6960-5 (pb)

ISBN 0-7445-7810-8 (pb)

ISBN 0-7445-6956-7 (pb)